DYLAN'S AMAZING DINOSAURS

THE SPINOSAURUS

To Lara and Ygraine – E.H.

For Maisie and Charlie – D.T.

SIMON AND SCHUSTER

First published in Great Britain in 2015 by Simon and Schuster UK Ltd • 1st Floor, 222 Gray's Inn Road, London WC1X 8HB • A CBS Company • Text copyright © 2015 E.T. Harper • Illustrations copyright © 2015 Dan Taylor • Paper engineering by Maggie Bateson • Concept © 2015 Simon and Schuster UK • The right of E. T. Harper and Dan Taylor to be identified as the author and illustrator of this work has been asserted by them in accordance with the Copyright, Designs and Patents Act, 1988 • All rights reserved, including the right of reproduction in whole or in part in any form • A CIP catalogue record for this book is available from the British Library upon request • ISBN: 978 1 4711 1938 5 • eBook ISBN: 978 1 4711 1939 2 • Printed in China • 10 9 8 7 6 5 4 3 2

DYLAN'S AMAZING DINOSAURS

THE SPINOSAURUS

E.T. HARPER AND DAN TAYLOR

SIMON AND SCHUSTER

London   New York   Sydney   Toronto   New Delhi

Dylan had an incredible tree house. It was full of fantastic things, and the most fantastic of all were Grandpa Fossil's magic Dinosaur Journal and . . .

Keep Out!

. . . WINGS, Dylan's toy pterodactyl!
He came to life whenever Dylan opened the journal and
they flew off on amazing adventures together to make
awesome dinosaur discoveries.

Dylan opened the journal to a page all about the spinosaurus.

Fact File
*Name: Spinosaurus
(Spine Lizard)
Size: bigger than a T. REX
Diet: mainly fish but also
giant herbivorous sauropods
(other big plant-eating
dinosaurs)
Habitat: Hot tropical swamps
Unusual features: Huge spiny
sail used for . . .*

Spinosaurus

'That's it, Wings! We need to find out what
its spiny sail is used for. That's our next dino mission!'

At the mention of a dino mission, Wings leapt to life, shook out his wings and flew out of the tree house.

'Let's go, let's soar . . . off to the land where the dinosaurs roar!' Dylan shouted.

They flew high and low over Roar Island, searching for a spinosaurus.
Soon they were over a swampy jungle where Dylan
thought he saw something between the trees.

He reached into his rucksack to find his binoculars,
but . . . oh no . . . he lost his grip on the shoulder strap!

The rucksack fell down through the trees.

'I have to get it back, Wings!' cried Dylan.
'Let's go lower . . .'

Wings dropped Dylan in the jungle, but before there
was a chance to look for the rucksack – CRASH!
'I spy a spinosaurus!' Dylan yelled.

Then he spotted something dangling from
the spinosaurus's gigantic jaws.

'He's got my rucksack!'

Wings and Dylan could only watch as the spinosaurus plunged its snout into the swampy water.

The dinosaur quickly resurfaced again, triumphantly shaking a giant fish in its massive jaws.

The rucksack was still tangled in its teeth.

'How are we ever going to get my rucksack back?' groaned Dylan.

Suddenly the spinosaurus caught sight of them.
'Quick! Into the swamp, Wings,' shouted Dylan. 'I've got an idea . . .'

SQUELCH!

They flew out covered in weeds and slime. 'Now we look like a scary swamp monster!' said Dylan.

'Fly round and round his head, Wings. If he tries to catch us, maybe the rucksack will fall out of his mouth,' Dylan called. They swooped round and, as they flew, huge globs of slimy weed dropped onto the spinosaurus's sail.

The dino was soon dizzy and it roared in frustration.
The rucksack fell from its jaws.

'Quick, let's go and get it,' shouted Dylan.

But they weren't quick enough. The fierce beast spotted them.

'GO WINGS!' Dylan shouted, glancing behind him
as the dino began to chase them.

But the spinosaurus suddenly slowed down. Its roars turned to whimpers. 'Hold on, Wings!' Dylan exclaimed. 'There's something wrong. It looks like a dog, panting. What's making it so hot? I wonder if it's got something to do with the slime on its sail? We need to wash it off. But how?'

As they were thinking, Dylan heard a rumbling, rushing sound
somewhere up ahead. 'Let's take a look, Wings!' he said.
And they flew high into the tree canopy.

There was the most beautiful waterfall Dylan had ever seen.
'Now we just need to lead it there,' said Dylan.

Dylan and Wings bravely flew near the slumped spinosaurus to get its attention. Even in its exhausted state, the huge predator couldn't resist. It lumbered after them all the way to . . .

The beautiful waterfall.

'Look! It's all right now. Washing off that slime has done the trick,' said Dylan. 'And now I think I understand what its sail is used for. Come on, Wings, time to go!'

They landed back safely in Dylan's tree house.

'That sail helps the spinosaurus keep its cool!' said Dylan. 'It's so big,
it helps spread out the heat. So when it was covered up with all
the slime and weeds, the dino overheated and couldn't run any more!'

Dylan closed the journal. 'Thanks for being so brave, Wings.

You may have been covered in slime, but you're certainly not weedy!'

Look out for more amazing adventures
with Dylan and Wings!

Out now -
The Tyrannosaurus Rex
The Stegosaurus

Coming soon -
The Triceratops